FOX WENT OUT ON A CHILLY NIGHT

FOX WENT OUT ON A CHILLY NIGHT

WENDY WATSON

LOTHROP, LEE & SHEPARD BOOKS   NEW YORK

First Edition   1   2   3   4   5   6   7   8   9   10

Library of Congress Cataloging in Publication Data
Watson, Wendy. Fox went out on a chilly night / by Wendy Watson.
p.   cm.   Summary: An illustrated version of the folk song in which a fox travels many miles to
get dinner for his wife and ten cubs.   ISBN 0-688-10765-6.—ISBN 0-688-10766-4 (lib. bdg.)
1. Folk songs, English—United States—Texts.   [1. Folk songs—United States.]   I. Title.
PZ8.3.W345Fo   1994   782.42162′13′00268—dc20   92-44157   CIP   AC

FOR JAMES

Fox went out on a chilly night

And he prayed to the moon to give him light—

He'd many a mile to go that night

Before he reached the town-o!

Town-o! Town-o!

Many a mile to go that night

Before he reached the town~o!

He ran 'til he came to a great big pen.

The ducks and geese were kept therein.

"One of you will grease my chin

Before the moon goes down-o!

Down-o! Down-o!

One of you will grease my chin

Before the moon goes down~o!"

He took the gray goose by the neck

And swung him right across his back.

He didn't mind the quack, quack, quack,

And the legs all dangling down-o!

    Down-o! Down-o!

He didn't mind the quack, quack, quack,

And the legs all dangling down-o!

Then old Mother Slipper-Slopper

jumped out of bed

And out of the window she popped her head.

She cried, "John, John, the gray goose is gone

And the fox is on the town-o!

Town-o! Town-o!

John, John, the gray goose is gone

And the fox is on the town-o!"

Then John he ran to the top of the hill

And he blew his horn both loud and shrill.

Fox he said, "Better flee with my kill,

For they'll soon be on my trail-o!

Trail-o! Trail-o!"

Fox he said, "Better flee with my kill,

For they'll soon be on my trail-o!"

Then Fox he ran to his cozy den
And there were his little ones,
eight, nine, ten.

They said, "Daddy, better go back again
For it must be a mighty fine town-o!

Town-o! Town-o!"
They said, "Daddy, better go back again
For it must be a mighty fine town-o!"

Then Fox and his wife, without any strife,

Cut up the goose with a carving knife.

They never had such a feast in their life,

And the little ones chewed on the bones-o!

Bones-o! Bones-o!

They never had such a feast in their life,

And the little ones chewed on the bones-o!

FOX WENT OUT ON A CHILLY NIGHT

(Traditional tune and words)

Fox went out on a chil - ly night, and he

prayed to the moon to give him light. He'd many a mile to

go that night Be - fore he reached the town - o!

Town - o! To - wn - o! Many a mile to

go that night, Be - fore he reached the town - o!